PRAISES FOR DAVID OMER BEARDEN

"*The Thing In Packy Innard's Place* was the last mature achievement that David lived to complete . . . He had language crackling through his cortex, and shimmering from his fingertips like a St. Elmo's fire of the soul. He occupied the essence of Poet. By the time he wrote *The Thing In Packy Innard's Place*, his poems had become transmogrified into paragraphs, but his paragraphs can hardly be regarded as prose. Meter there was truly his march to a different drummer."

— *Dion Wright*

"In his final work, David Bearden casts a "dure-eye" on the barflies of a local tavern that he frequented and a sympathetic one on the denizens of the homeless shelter where he worked. The result is *The Thing In Packy Innard's Place*—a work of high fantasy informed by an affinity for the quotidian. As a stranger in their midst Bearden's narrator evokes a hypnagogic vision of the lives of the people of Scranton, Pennsylvania as well as the city's history and natural environs."

— *Robert Dumont*

"*The Thing In Packy Innard's Place* certainly has a place among experimental, avant-garde writings both for his evident broad acquaintance with various contemporary, at the time, cultural nuances and events, as well as his embrace of literally funky world spaces. I can dig from that read why he would have admired Lamantia because there is more than a trace of neo-surrealistic prose to find in his made language."

— *Gerd Stern*

BOOKS BROUGHT OUT BY
ROSACE PUBLICATIONS

———

ANTHOLOGIES

LE FEU DU CIEL (1965) Chapbook

SMOKING MIRROR (1974) Chapbook

BY DAVID OMER BEARDEN

SO LONG AT THE FAIR & DOWN AT THE PALOMINO CLUB
& OTHER POEMS (1976) Chapbook

THE ROSACE IN A STAR CHAMBER (1981) Chapbook

REDRESS (1983) Chapbook

THE MENTAL TRAVELER (2018) Poetry Book

THE THING IN PACKY INNARD'S PLACE (2019) Novel

BY ALAN BÄTJER RUSSO

DOMINION AND OTHER POEMS (1977) Chapbook

STATE LINE (Forthcoming) Collected Writings

BY DION WRIGHT

TEMPUS FUGITIVE (2016) Memoir of the 60s

ZIP AREA (Forthcoming) Correspondence Book

the**Thing**

In Packy Innard's Place

DAVID OMER BEARDEN

ROSACE
Publications

An excerpt from this story, in different form, appeared in
Welcoming Hands, the Catholic Social Services Newsletter.
Roskilde's Ballad appeared in *The Villager*,
a newspaper published in Roaring Brook township, PA.

Rafael Lemkin (1900-1959) was a special advisor at the
Nuremberg War Guilt Trials. He gave us the word "Genocide."
Frank Belknap Long (1903-1992) wrote *The Hounds of Tindalos*,
a paradigm of the *"Aliens from Another Dimension"* tale.

Roundup into manuscript completed 2007.
First edition published in the United States in 2019 by Rosace Publications.

Book design and edited by Astra Beck

Cataloging-in-Publication Data is available from the Library of Congress

Printed in the United States of America
Library of Congress Control Number: 2019940721
ISBN 978-0-9997777-1-8 (paperback)

www.rosacepublications.com

ACKNOWLEDGMENTS

Heart font gratitude to Astra Beck,
who designed this book and cover, believed in it,
and provided constant help and support.

Thanks also to Edward C. Evarts, William Beck,
Theresa Beck, Johanna Beck, Aaron Kemble,
James Bearden, Staci Moser, Jeannette Mallozzi,
Bob Bailey, Robert Dumont and Dion Wright.

TO ASTRA BECK

Here's a little fable,
Astra Jane, for your light on my life

* * *

CONTENTS

FOREWORD

———

The Thing In Packy Innard's Place is a requiem to all the lost souls falling like snow at the end of James Joyce's, *The Dead*. It is a requiem to David Omer Bearden's life told in apocalyptic images of beautiful honesty. It reminds me of the scene at the end of the film Amadeus where the composer from his death bed cries out the final, angelic notes of his own requiem as death coils around him like a noose. David's work is not only elegiac but deeply empathetic. It is a celebration of the people that you may see on the street and look away from in fear or shame, the people who have fallen between the cracks of society. David so beautifully captures each of the people he cares for at a homeless shelter in elevated language worthy of Joyce; he creates his own kind of heightened vernacular which mixes the homeless "rainacular shelta" and his own poetic myth making. He creates images of spellbinding beauty; a moment where he plays a Bee Gees tune on the jukebox only for the publican to reach around the back of the machine and hit the reject button; and the cat that wanders into the bar and begins to judge each of the patrons like an Egyptian deity. How can one forget the heartbreaking moment David, sickened with hepatitis C, returns to Packy Innard's for a Busch he is too sick to drink? He encounters the microscopic hands of a winter fly and his countenance turns into the Sutton Hoo helmet. There is a beautiful moment where David is cooking fish fillets for the homeless in his care and prepares the meal with the devotion of a parent. He captures these moments in language of such empathy, it gives each resident at the shelter a heroic quality as they wrestle between neoteny and death. I think David's work functions in a similar way to Charles Dickens' novels; it gives a kind of nobility to the homeless that society has taken from them. There is a moment in the novel where David looks at the bar through the eyes of his father, it is a moment of elevation, of sadness and honesty, that permeates through the whole work. Great writing like this makes us look through another person's eyes, it humbles us to know that the same place looks different depending on who is looking. This is the essence of empathy. *The Thing In Packy Innard's Place* is not only David's last work, but a maturation of David's entire career; his love of images, his love of ancient heroic works and his constant struggle with his demons and his guilt, through language that is captivating and poetic. In the final, mysterious passage of the novel, David's work echoes the ending of James Joyce's *The Dead* when he speaks of how; "He listened to the alarming, silent clock of snow in yards, on roofs, drifting in gutters over all Westward," and I think of how David's work is filled with allusions but is entirely his own vernacular, as if the language itself is his shelter from the storm. *The Thing In Packy Innard's Place* moves me to tears; it is a tender requiem to the wounded and the sad.

— *Nicholas Tolkien*

EDITOR'S PREFACE

———

For the last fifteen years of David Omer Bearden's life, he lived in Scranton, Pennsylvania. He worked at various jobs before becoming the night manager and caretaker for the residents of the St. Anthony's Haven Shelter. While off-duty he embraced service work by carrying sandwiches with him to give out to the homeless when he walked around town. He also devoted much of his time to schmoozing and observing the scene in a local bar called Pat Langan's, which inspired his final work: *The Thing* In Packy Innard's Place*. The title derives from the Sicilian Mafia term Cosa Nostra (Our Thing) and "Innard's" alludes to the guts of the place. It is a hard book to classify. Picaresque? Satire? High-fantasy? Dystopian fiction with elements of the quotidian? The novel clearly is not of a conventional type and greatly challenged his creative powers during the five years he spent writing it.

At this time in David's life, he was suffering from the effects of Hepatitis C. He had contracted this disease while working at the homeless shelter after being accidentally punctured by a syringe that was left on a sofa by one of the residents. Though he came to realize his condition would sooner or later be fatal, he opted not to consider drastic medical interventions and passed away in 2008, a year after completing *The Thing In Packy Innard's Place*.

I worked closely with David on laying out his last mature piece of writing and making his edits. This process often took days because we communicated almost exclusively via snail mail as e-mail was not easily accessible for him. I would visit David frequently on the weekends—traveling from New Jersey to Pennsylvania with the revised proofs. I always looked forward to our morning breakfasts spent listening to classical music while conversing about different lines in the book and what they meant.

I learned quickly that this book was not an easy read; one sentence felt like one paragraph. Quite often there was no way I could get past a sentence without looking up several words in the dictionary. Nevertheless, I found his use of obscure words and clever puns to be perfectly placed with microscopic skill, their order displaying a rooted sense of rhythm and meaning.

The book reminded me of a painting, with layers upon layers of texture, color, and imagery. Each re-reading of it seemed to reveal a different storyline. When it came time to take photos for the book, David took me inside Pat Langan's bar. It was like walking into someone's living room. I'd never experienced anything like it. Everything he had described in the book sprang to life and came at me at hyperspace speed! I realized that his sensitivity in transcribing his surroundings was truly brilliant in the way it provided a keen perspective on the people and environs of Scranton, and on mankind itself.

David also wrote a shorter, more reader-friendly version called *Pat Langan's Place* that was meant for the actual bar patrons. Even though the second version was not intended to be a prologue, I felt it completed the novel and was conducive to a broader understanding of its theme that because of the book's complexity, a reader might initially have difficulty grasping.

As David was a stepfather to me and left me in care of his work when he passed away, it was only in the matter of divine time to have finally published his last greatest piece of writing, *The Thing In Packy Innard's Place*. I'm honored to share this book now with the literary community and be a part of preserving his legacy.

— Astra Beck

** The Thing also is a reference to the Althing—the Icelandic National Parliament— which is the oldest parliamentary body in existence. David could have been alluding to the general tendency of the denizens of these old man Irish bars to hold forth at great length on any and every topic under the sun in an attempt to solve the world's problems. A parliamentary gathering of sorts. The Cosa Nostra/Our Thing allusion also works so it's a double-barreled multilingual pun.*

NOTES BY AN OLD FRIEND

Astra Beck has revealed the way the poet David Omer Bearden died. It makes me grind my teeth with frustration at the needlessness of it. He had been running a homeless shelter in Scranton, Pennsylvania. One night cleaning up the premises, he was straightening out the cushions on a sofa when he got stuck by a carelessly discarded needle left there, and contracted Hep-C from it. I imagine him knowing in that biting instant that he'd been mortally had. His brother James says he heard from David by phone about then, and he knew that he was doomed. He kept on writing and revising.

David lived with survivor guilt his entire life, yielding sometimes to behavior that increased that guilty conscience. He was of Southern Baptist red-neck roots, but not peasant roots. My theory is that he came from highly evolved stock caught in economically reversed circumstances. I believe that he suffered his survivor-guilt in consequence of the death of his infant twin brother. Being the survivor lay corrupting at the bottom of his early childhood psychology, and colored everything from then on.

David was an autodidact, and also owned a brilliant mind possessing a formidable talent. He had the tap wide open all the time, and the verbiage poured out steadily throughout his entire life. Maybe nobody since James Joyce has loved language as much as Dave did. I think he may also have had an eidetic memory; at least he was never at a loss for words. However abstruse and unexpected, even incomprehensible, his juxtapositions were, they were always true, and would eventually reveal their essence.

He was also the owner of a human sweetness we rarely encounter, which I think may have sometimes embarrassed him. Then he might snap into vexation and get angry, but never cruel. David was very sympathetic, and not one to inflict pain. . . although he sometimes did so, in pursuit of his Muse. His rages were brief, and defensive in nature, being inauthentic gestures to cover up his empathy, and which may have sometimes worried him to feel was unmanly.

With regard to his formal writing, he revised and revised and revised. No average person could keep up. I aways thought that his first statements were inspired and not in need of improvement, but he was a devotee of perfectibility. He and his close friend, the "Wichita Vortex" poet, Alan Russo, were in perfect mental harmony where they overlapped, and where they diverged, each was plagued by personal daemons. Such people yearn for human contact, but make the relationships they form stressful for the others who love them.

In what I suppose was a sort of effort to expiate his sins, real or imaginary, Dave eventually devoted himself to the welfare of others, but he never quit writing. His final relationships were solid. When he found out he had Hep-C, he refused treatment. I guess he thought he deserved his fate, even though treatment had been developed. Ambivalent, ambiguous and frightening, he smiled sweetly and climbed up onto his cross.

His magnum opus, and his final work, *The Thing In Packy Innard's Place*, is a dense evocation of a disappeared world and the human creatures who inhabited it.

> *— Dion Wright*
> *David Omer Bearden's friend for half a century*

*"I believe the only news of any interest
does not come from the great cities or from
the councils of state, but from some lonely
watcher on the hills who has a momentary
glimpse of infinitude and feels the
universe rushing at him."*

— A.E.'S LETTERS TO MÍNANLÁBÁIN

PROLOGUE

———

PAT LANGAN'S PLACE

A globally warm, future, spring day in sleepy Slocum Hollow. Her little silver Vespa easily topped the sunny hill, & eased down the alley called Soldier's Court to where it debouched onto cracked & pot-holed Lafayette Street. A metallic chirring came far away.

Standing astride for a nano-moment, she gazed toward the pickled saltbox on the corner, remembering when she, as a child, dutifully braved that noisy place with a folded newspaper, silently, shyly accepting payment from merry Mr. Langan, his proferred dollar (now extinct) often covering a Reese's peanut butter cup (also extinct) or other delicious treats. Then mutely vanishing away, to go & peddle her papers. (The Scranton Times, now defunct).

Now she was a tall, sun-buff, purposeful beauty, with raven tresses rather loosely tucked up under a fetching pith helmet, a bright paisley bandana adorning her khaki quarry shirt, wheat jeans tight on womanly legs, tucked into polished cordovan engineer's boots.

Smiling privately with nostalgia, she also took in a ruined arbor across the way, where a weathered "Zumbo's Pizza" sign clung to the ghost of a trellised estaminet.

Glided, then, over to the old Langan's Place; cracked, vine-scrawled now, patched. A dim, peach-blow neon paraph spelled out "Shebeen" in a window. Doorsteps choked with pachysandra.

She slipped into the pub darkness, momentarily blinded, as of old, wiping her radiantly sweaty face with her bright bandana.

Leaning confidently on the bar, she addressed the black

bartender first telepathically; then, receiving no waves back, vocally ordered a beer.

"Only cognac available today madam," announced the blue-black barman, wiping the counter before her.

"I must apologize, Madam, My colleague, Mr. Patel, seems to have sold off the entire beer allotment. I am Mr. Nwakile."

Smiling a wide white smile reminiscent of Tiger Woods, he poured for her a shot of what appeared to be well brandy.

"When this was Mr. Langan's place, he served only beer," she smiled, recalling the odd, blond skunk odor, the bleary old men with their beer cans clumsily cajoling her.

She remembered one old white-haired telepath who could commune wordlessly with her, unnoticed, of course, by the rest of the beer-blotted crew loudly talking over one another.

She sipped her glass of what Mr. Nwakile hyperbolically referred to as "Hennessy," & asked politely after a world gone:

"Do any white westsiders come in here any more?"

Mr. Nwakile considered a moment, & replied

"The old paisar who has pickles, & Miss Donna Rose, though Mr. Patel, who comes in evenings, may know better than I, for the old ones mostly come out at night."

"I'm off," she pronounced. *"Please mention my visit to Mr. Petal; I may be back some evening.*

I am a pseudozoanist, Mr. Nwakile. I venture into the DeNaples barrens, beyond Updike Hollow, to observe the life cycle of metallobioforms. You know, those segmented tin bugs from who knows where that eat the black hills of tires in there, leaving those lacy black rings you must have seen on the ground?"

"Yes, Madam. & then, Madam?"

"Well, Mr. Nwakile I think I'll hover over to the Isle of Frog & Toe. They tell me that there, gigantic otters frolic down the smooth glass sides melted out from the skyscraper windows during the Apocalypse. I mean to sort of join them, & record their splashings over the sunken city for the environmentalists of Marywood College."

Then she waved a beautiful, graceful adios, mounted her silver Vespa, & glided away.

Who knows if she ever returned?

STAVE I

Where present hour honking Lackawanna Avenue & Adams Avenue cross, was once owl quaver wilderness. Then by & by Ebeneezer & Benjamin, the Slocum brothers, cleared a spot there to raise sheep. Depredations of lank wolves & big cats slinking from out the deep tamarack swamp finished off their poor flock. A long khaki field of wheat grew where Lackawanna Station now stands. A Mr. Howe sold the Slocum boys a grist mill there, in 1797. The Slocums wanted to call the site Unionville, instead of Dark Hollow, which the settlers called it, from the contour of those, endless hills & vales, with that old breeze through a dense weald of pine, towering spruce, & larches. So somehow the neighborhood around the grain mill & distillery business became known as Slocum Hollow, & homeboys rode mules up to the still to fill a jug with usquebaugh. By 1828 the village of Slocum Hollow was slumbering in decay.

They call this neighborhood Westside, & I feel it a part of greater Slocum Hollow; a neck of the woods, a village, a tribal community. Now this felt Westside, vicinage in area, extends roughly from the fly sprent black screen door of Bill Shiree's beer garden there on Main Street, up to tidy Bernie's bar on the corner of Jackson, & up the hill to be capped on the corner of Everett & Lafayette by Pat Langan's Place, at the foot of West Mountain. Within & around this imaginary (& somewhat arbitrary), triangle, is found the centripetal street life of mom & pop grocery stores like Brunetti's & Vitalies', more taverns, like Bigsy's & Paul's, & one no-name joint on Swettland I pass often but have never entered, & village pedestrian movement. Listless piano practice may occasionally be barely heard.

So. Mister Pat Langan presides over a little bar on the corner of Everett & Lafayette streets in the Westside of Scranton, Pennsylvania. As Johanna & I moved into this house, I looked up & noticed the white, blue-bronze glowing pastel sign that said LANGANS (drink Royal Crown Cola); – I never knew anyone to do that; we drink beer in Pat's! & the neon signs glowing orange & blue out of the corner of my eye, & the store-front windows painted in a child's hand with beer mugs & shamrocks, & I thought "maybe!"

O yeah. First I checked out the larger drinking establishment catty-corner across the way. The vibe in there seemed somber though; that dismal Pennsylvania paranoid reserve with little of the leaven of raucous voices & laughter (Roy gulls), Mark braying laughter like a good humor mule. . . I always heard in Pat's threshold on my way to catch the Drinker bus across Scrantonstady to work at the grim basement shelter in a hollow like war-disheveled Bosnia, thinly populated with skinny, slow down & outers, like Kosovar Dalmatians. . .

STAVE II

"I am hand and glove with all sorts of fanciers,
spital-field weavers and all sorts of odd specimens
of the Human species, who fancy Pigeons"
— Charles Darwin

When the Copenhagen blue sky goes a deep bruise, like an old kitsch postcard of nostalgia & regret, over the gothic turrets of what I think of as Lackawanna bridge Glyptoxthek, & the vermeil gilt onion of the basilica, gleaming after rain, perhaps you may have a glimpse of him; an old black silhouette on a certain street corner in bornite twilight & pale street lights just fluttering on, regarding the beauteous ladies of the evening coming from the mirth of the Melba Bar, to slip wetly past on the Drinkerstrasse. . . See him, perhaps atrociously shaken by memory, & clutching a black umbrella, or is it a walking cane?

I walk on in to a workplace I'll tell you about, through streets from which the sense of ease, cheerfulness, & spontaneity is vanishing. . . or is it me?

Well, winter is getting here. A cold breeze swells beneath a moving blue & black leopardskin sky, portentous of snow.

I find the keys on the board, enter the back way, grab a sackful of fish fillets from the freezer, & lay them out on an oven tray.

Professionally cheering up, I flip on the Arbus-eyed monitor &

set up for the night, putting out the hopeful stack of white towels.

Marisol Rosaura is shivering at the door. I click her on in, followed immediately by Kaspar Hauser[1], rowdy old Micajah Harpe[2], & a few of the boys from the Burgess Shale[3] camp on the river.

About a baker's dozen tonight; plenty of fish to go around. Set out with loaves, supper commences.

Set the television on low, so as to absorb talk from the soylent couch as I tend to duties. . . overheard how in the sky, faint stars are crushed like roses in a bible, into black holes. They say that frogs, with their sensitive skins, are disappearing all over the world. . .

I impose a little order on the belongings closet. Rich will do his Augean thing in there, come Saturday.

Let me review Rich's log entries. I've come to appreciate his style.

Jerry has somehow retrieved Marisol's lost luggage. She's pleased, & avers that Jerry owns & operates a heart of gold. There is some evidence for this.

Marisol has found a job. Since she is working, I'll hold the same bed for her. I'll attempt to interview old Micajah tonight, if I can make sense out of him. Jeff taught me the armature of this job: to hold out a firm welcoming hand.

Called in, from far Westside, I'm learning this mission: to actually implement their Christs' social teachings with compassionate diligence.

Human or alien warmth passed hand to hand in St. Anthony's Haven, mens' & womens' shelter, on a street of Scranton, down here far below the gridlocked traffic of the homeless stars.

STAVE III

So one morning I poured myself off the rattletrap bus, plumb tuckered out vibratile & frazzled from the bizarre all nighter I'd just pulled (*"That's not really a job"* Somebody opined along the bar. Hardest job I ever held down.), & strayed on into Pat's place for a beer. Maybe this little beer joint will be in the old-fashioned human tradition I was nostalgically trying to find here in this, to me, strange eastern region custom I knew as a boy from The Shamrock Bar in my hometown, where one found one's father passing out checks to his work crew on lost Friday nights, in a distant western land, a long time ago.[4]

In a lot of ways, it was. A speckled trout flapped slapping on a wall plaque. A cheerful gopher rocked singing *"I'm all right,"* a little chap with a cactus for a dick stood in a vase listening to a gorilla do an Elvis hit. (Hunka Hunka Burnin' Love) A brace of bakelite bulldogs woofed & a porcelain bast meowed. I was a Bladerunner entering delirium tremens. Dreaming of these white Christians. The heavy, calm publican was alert & friendly from in front, & very knowledgeable of his blue-collar, working-man clientele, & well, charismatic in the Irish way. His judgments became law in there organically; natural as a grapevine.

Then one fine day another stray sauntered into Pat Langan's place. A strapping marmalade, no, tortoiseshell, no, brindle cats from out an alley somewhere. A mysterious being, as all cats are, & a stranger, like myself.[5] I don't want to call it either a tom or a pussy, for Lucky is a he-she, alien & self-contained beyond any name she might be given. Lucky beyond the lady; no Buddhist, but Buddha, the gunslinger gunslingers dread. I affirm that, while everybody advised Pat about this interloping isolato according to his nature; those who cottoned to Lucky got a lot of points in my book; those who advised having Lucky extradited or even put to death I noted well, as those whom Lucky was averse to earned my dubiety too. So we all keep our own council, Pat, Lucky, & myself, respectively, & belly up to the bar. Still, who in Langan's save Pat & myself, are right ailurophiles?

From the outset I enjoyed by Pat's imprimatur the fair tolerance of the guys I came to know in Pat's place, who otherwise would have been ever more reticent toward an outlander long hair poet, I'm convinced if you aren't.

Slide a packet of Camels down the bar toward Mike Moran, & indulge myself in the strange & ridiculous pleasure of regaining Mr. Dixon's goodwill, from scratch. Walk the triangle with mad Primich, & ditch him in Shiree's. Swap jokes with Maddy & Betty. Frank the barkeep I brought a peace offering of pearl onions. *"What's this?"* Just pearl onions in a futile cream sauce, for terminal scepticism. Freddy is salty, & all hands mortally curious as to my work hours (24/7), my status vis-à-vis Johanna, my ultimate provenance, etc., but under Pat's star, I made contingent friends. Some good ones, to be sure.

Pat gave me a hand getting a garden in. He had a rototiller borrowed from Coach, which we used to plow up a little strip in the backyard, Pat laughing in wonder that I raised a sweat. Planted peppers of two kinds, jalapeño & some other kind, tomatoes, & good summer squash. I presented Pat the first yield of this garden, a monster zucchini. Can anyone in here explain why green bell peppers are called "mangoes" around these parts? Mark presented me a mess of spiced tripe, which I cooked with hominy to make menudo for the hangover victims at the shelter. Noted everyman's views on the influx of Philly blacks into the region.

One night Pat & I were discussing many things. How in say an half a century this pub & all in it will be gone & forgotten. Maybe not. Down the bar butch & Cheryl squabble amiably about Glen's acclaimed pickles. Pat wondered aloud why Zimmie doesn't retire. I should have quoted him this versicle, but I didn't think to:

> *"don't carry dead weight,*
> *ain't no flash in the pan;*
> *alright I'll set ya straight,*
> *can't you see I'm a union man. . ."*
> *— Bob Dylan*

I squint over the brim of my beer to notice on Pat's impassive countenance the all-encompassing 100-yard beer stare my old man employed to take in an entire room, & all the gabbling denizens, & Donny's plumbing skills, Jim McGraw's Yankee handiman expertise, & each & every conversation. It is an underwater gaze, fixed on nobody in particular, dreaming but conscious, & I believe infallible in its clairvoyance. I too am subject to go into this gaze, in order to take the bright overview. Nobody notices.[6]

That old icebox white van, with the Steelers spare tire cover, rambles up Lafayette, down to Bernie's, back around the triangle, past Bigsy's on to check out his sister Esther in Shiree's Lounge, wanders on, on toward stops unknown to me, the VFW maybe. That would be Roy, & you know you're in Westside.

Joe Matyjevich called Pat at the bar, from Paris! In an access of severe, intransigent homesickness. Didn't even hit the street, stayed in his hotel room over there. No Champs Élysées, no Place Pigalle. No place like Westside, n'est-ce pas?

The bar is loaded with blurring convives. Frank gets off, dons his ball cap, & joins some colossal crows in the lineup near the corner of the room. The Varmint holds forth to me of Bremerton & Seattle. I suggest we make a run out there one of these days. I know that rainy country well. The ship canal in Puget Sound. The skies there are bruise blue, & agony peach. Shafts of silver strike the sound. I see Ralph doesn't hear me; he is crossing his beer meridian. Pat, please get him & Roy another beer, & me yet one more. I feel better already.

Outside, high over Lafayette Street, noctilucent clouds pale & pull apart, revealing, near Nellie's Court, a well-rounded individual walking a waterlogged dog; preserving a stability & identity once provided by the original Slocum Hollow, the ur-patch, founded in sweat, then left to evolve spontaneously. Taller than wide gothic row houses with ruby tomato gardens in the valley of the world.

I like it here in Pat Langan's place. I noticed a blue clock, shimmering like a stargate, near the back door, where Lucky's tapeta show iridescent in the gloom.

Let's imagine Slocum Hollows, any number of them, in infinite manifestation where rainbows go to ground somewhere in the endless mountains, peaks on which one or two improbable emissaries stand watching, while a vast cauliflower ear of cloud listens in on Westside.

Beer all around.

1. See: Werner Herzog's film *Every Man for Himself and God Against All: The Enigma of Kasper Hauser.*

2. Harpe, William Micajah (aka Big), older of two murderous homeless brothers on the Barren River. He was beheaded by a posse in 1799.

3. See: *Wonderful Life: The Burgess Shale and The Nature of History,* by Stephen Jay Gould.

4. *"Only through losing our place in this overlapping circle of wombs, can we attain to that ultimate pattern where childhood selects its running wing and grave."*

   — Kenneth Patchen,
   CONTINUATION OF THE LANDSCAPE

5. *"'Tis no disparagement to be a stranger, or so irksome to be an exile. The rain is a stranger to the earth, rivers to the sea, Jupiter in Egypt, the Sun to us all. The Soul is an alien to the Body, a Nightingale to the air, a swallow in an house, and Ganymede in Heaven, an elephant at Rome, a Phoenix in India; and such things commonly please us best which are most strange, and come farthest off."*

   — Robert Burton,
   THE ANATOMY OF MELANCHOLY

6. Karl Pribram proposed a *"frequency realm from which our brain mathematically constructs its reality,"* viewing the brain as a micro-hologram of the macro-hologram of the universe.

   Russel Targ proposed that we *"live in a kind of holographic soup, closer in time-space than a naive realism allows."*

   "Whatever we call reality, it is revealed to us only through the active construction in which we participate."

   — Ilya Prigogine

OCK
Budweiser
IRISH EYES
WILL BE SMILING
LANGANS

SECTION ONE

"If we could only get inside
of Area 51, say the townspeople of Rachel –
population 91 – we could save the aliens,
and thus save ourselves.
In the meantime, at least, we know
that they are near."

— JOHN D' AGATA, HALLS OF FAME

The Roskilde *(Larvatus Prodeo)* traveler had something to assoil, you know, when he wandered down the unraveling trace from stony Zealand in the insensate still after midnight, into the closed and shuttered city of Awoken. Strewn derelict across Sovere Hollow in the endless mountains, over the blue-gray Pococurantish chain, under the knob of Mount Plymlymon.

In preterite life he had come to quicklime light as a specimen of roaster guinea pig (neotenous, to be sure) or abrogable yellow tadpole in the pond of the human hand.

Desistantly walking on, Roskilde neatly remembered how around that fatal hour, the hottest horror-bull from Churlemagne *(Habemus Papem Terrible)* mandated that all must go drivingly upbeat; the get-hot-or-get-out deal: Patriots of Zealand! Suffer not a loser, beautiful to plug-ugly or fairy-floss-fair. No inconsolable background music. No *fados*; to hell with viral blues people, moonlit and snotty. Nary a tear better undertake to drop down and out. Trump a chump unto towering Churlemagne. No yokel of constant sorrow need apply. Cancel brimming, terminal shanty eyes. Poor wayfaring stranger, shit out of luck. Victory prevails. Seal affixed, painted shut.

Well, Roskilde got pinched. His nerve got pinched. Busted, landed in the high street by angling hoplites of the beastmaster; dragged under close arrest to tedious inquisition in a bone-rigged hall by that same Churlemagne, before his side-kick Regulus, their godis and lictors and deputies.

Under proclamation of Nithing, stuck in the side, rendered obsolete, out of space, shunned, separated, transported. Sent packing by the same *Althing* of eternity (convoked for that occasion on a certain island; not of the blessed, really, nor mangrove pirate key, just the Isle of Frog and Toe, where mortal blue hunks of ice crash to the streets from sky-scraping spires; factory-farm hives of the *have* people.)

The bona fide, densely, perdurably incarnate gang turning out a gangrel of "an unearthly extreme of androgynous male beauty," (wagging quasar to tinseltown asteroid) but blighted, purely blighted. Off-white tumbler of bonnyclabber, alkali rose martian dust devil. Man like a buttermilk sky.

Implacable Churlemagne sanctioned and smeared Roskilde as a shit across the heavens while Roskilde, deep down in his inner sky, knew better; he felt who the *real* shits were, having learned over several lifetimes of being singled out by the genuine article, on three worlds.

Blown from harbor through grisly, jeopardous suburbs of avocatory night, his involuntary will to live under wraps (Kafka's dipnoan lungs) among the natural Nazis occupying those Netherlands, it finally dawned on Roskilde he'd really been invalided out from that horde of homininety, that human race. Then the north-eastern hollows yawned ad hoc for him, strange and pristine as asymmetrical mazzard saplings in some cherry valley, remote crossroads more exotic than Tuzla Oklahoma, the sad populace outlandish, their convenances utterly droll; no place or anyone familiar. This oddly revived him, like prospect; like resilient, mint-condition neoteny. Borne at all adventure, in outer darktowns where the dreaded worst had already happened, some while ago.

He worked, jack of trades, as a carpenter's helper, a tour guide, (shucking in the past tense), a printer's courier, a front desk clerk jiving in a subjunctive mood at Mt. Carny Resort, insensibly coming to almost love his wound (the Astrobleme), if it opened him into a children's circle of shining space; fulgurant disclosure of raw freedom and absurd joy. Churlemagne's manwich and virus cup of trembling.

At last Roskilde found called employment on a street of Awoken, in a homeless shelter, as a kind of beadle, or havenkeeper. A social worker, out in the cold.

A deep, abyssal breeze rose in him, with a funny light at the end of a wandering wand, to wrangle the fond and slow (turtledoves) with, and to shepherd the displaced into fold. As a probe, he would look for neoteny right here. He remembered how the first to go plumb evil on Churlemagne's thing were its serious, hotdogging, upwardly mobile adult players; its yuppies, whom he called the Borg.

Now he worked for a Catholic Borg outfit, staffed by ex-chorister boys and girls with the usual institutional complement of *geneurs*.

At incept, Roskilde amiably confided to beadledom his views concerning what was laughingly referred to as the floating weeds in their care, (once he tried to discuss the Branch Davidians but quickly saw he was among micro-arugula or mini-rocket yuppies in a chilly crisper, so switched to glib clicking in high-technophilic; that digerati's manifesto and gestalten the computer; proteomics, the global hotting up, top secrete teutonism or something, Evo Devo, telesis for strings and so on, and drew, in cartoon fustian, sophomoric little rebuses:

> *"How many social workers does it take to change a light bulb?"*
> *"Okay, how many?"*
> *"Just one, but the bulb has got to want to change."*)

Roskilde grew fluent in ebonics, rainacular shelta, and more and more often was called upon to dish out his unique caseation of macaronic spanish. He got on with relating to the urticate, scapegrace street tuberoses and rubble as he saw fit; covering in an idiolect current with his colleagues, (who were surely not digital talking point automatons), his posthuman mission: to linger awhile, reckoning at the fractal city limits of all relationships, in the landscape of estrangement, with the man who wasn't there.

*"Got a fixed position, but no abode, dog.
You've opted to pass without doing your social ticket;
one thing out of the way! About sour apples;
with your bad self, you're bound to get beat to death,
then thrown in jail, or vice versa. You need to chill.
Just stay out in the country a lot. In your shack there
below Jinglebob Camp. Yeah I've been down there. But look,
Quinn's in town. Get on the truck to frog hollow and
harvest pears with Francisquito and them."*

The urbanite sociologist *thing* adjudged Roskilde semi-savvy, but imponderable. From the south, they reasoned.

The seasoned bums in his care, more sensitive to the meta-message, noticed that what was humorous about macho Roskilde was not fatuous in him and loved him for that. Roskilde, for his part, knew a good separatist skell appreciates the humor in unilateral humiliation.

He still loved the range of practical uses in the complex idea of Machismo, with its riders and tack, husbanding the cattle of poverty in hieratic mime, posturing, frowning kabuki like a kid at the galactic pickup wheel, feeling the sintered, yet un-shuddering stator. He did good.

Roskilde's rapport with the unruly, ergot-poisoned droves was just beyond the conversation. They simply knew his good will was not the cupronickel slug and pistareen chickenfeed doled them by the social scientists of the Borg.

*"You all that, for real for real;
You are the Rose of San Antone up in this piece, man.
Naw, I'm the radish of sweet badish up in here.
You ain't said shit.
Laughter."*

Maybe he could change things, among these feral patsies with nothing to lose. He realized these had become as little strayaway children, in routed affright. He nightly overcame the sum of his own green fears, witnessed by all hands.

The waking Realization, of no moment to winners (in their armor, dog-eared from laconic prying eyes), was in that basement Roskilde's balancing, moving assemblage point. His revenant authenticity, with the compassion of a young mother behind the persona worn like an old (stutson) milk white hat in getting the job done, was for souls in pain, the poor, and exercised powers of healing at the borders of slotlessness. Spontaneous drift from havingness. Salvation? Drift. He suffered fools, and some he taught to be glad they weren't him.

Gabby has composed a poem, slyly handed to Roskilde in the shapeup. Here is what it said:

> *"It's a comsfarasee*
> *to lead your hart*
> *and soul away*
> > *with bad karma*

> *To fuck your*
> *bruzed pitiful*
> *being to death*

> *could you*
> *emagen a better*
> *or moor fitting death*
> > *Ol Horr."*

What characterized the bio-curve of the genpoor; brief, flaming youth, then, in time, glands choked, damping, dumbing down midway in a dark wood, was matched in the tragedy of neoteny; fresh *(ros geal dubh)* rosace or rosaleen blushing out into unprecedented air, under dab-hand (or cack-handed) indictment by patriot troops of consensus reality; by ape brow beaten til the petals fall. Downed airmen, lost and found on the ground, beneath carnivorous blue orchids, where roses cling in vain. Beauteous litter rotting on a floor jungled with baby penis worms listening to bassoons. But some blossom through, don't they?

Roskilde and Mare shared an apartment in the larynx of Plum-Head Alley. Red late afternoon meander in to work along a bloody clinker-buttressed old railroad embankment *(tin cans, dog-eared, ovoid-mouthed rolls of tarpaper, and there, like a big bullfrog on the pachysandra underneath the bushy euonymus, Hemingway's heavy liver, laminate of mahogany and lignum vitae)* and across Batterman, to the shelter in front of which there were usually a few homeless loitering like Turks at the gates of Vienna to speak to him before opening hour (7:30 p.m.).

Not quite pretty, plump Barbelo Marmeladova, of Sheol's rag trade, in street pancake and runway do, slouches near the entrance, huddled in covert conversation with the mulberry mug of Micajah Harpe, complotting with that timeworn swindler about how to chisel another night off the obdurate rock of shelter policy, no doubt, by way of Roskilde's bleeding heart. Easy to deal with. See if a break can't be cut, unbusted. Old sinister Gabby, leering toothlessly, in an incredibly filthy and bulbous in front Elsinore jacket (encinta with the baby of Rosemary Hayes, thought Roskilde), sidles up, to put in his ineffectually evil two cents worth.

The Copenhagen-blue sky is going a deep bruise, like a turn of the century postcard of unutterable nostalgia, over the shingled-roof row houses along these cairene courts and alleys, conical gothic turrets of what Roskilde (unfortunate traveler who couldn't be done) saw as the Drubinick glyptothek, barnlike spelter silk mills back of the depot, more drab businesses and gray rows of clapboard houses, then the vermeil gilt onion atop the Greek Orthodox basilica gleaming after rain. Get a load of the beset Antonite there; a lost silhouette who has gone the extra mile to this street corner under bornite twitterlight inlaid with pale flavescent sodium vapor lamps just fluttering on, mindful, ecstatic, disabused, from chaperoning lucid grief down bald streets of the mocked and wounded, where the mother of God is the bride of Frankenstein.

Mare had been crossing the river into Westward; vacuuming and scrubbing a little two-story Moesian house, taller than wide, on Field Lane. Plum-Head Alley was a slum. Westward was a decent working class neighborhood, I guess.

Roskilde and Mare were quarreling the day they moved from the alley and crossed the Achingrun, toward where the sun sets behind the hollow.

The former coal miner's narrow house sat three or four clones down in the row from a weather-seasoned salt box on the corner, where high, buffed and rebuffed by blustery winds, a purplish pink, faintly glowing pastel plastic tavern sign made known Innard's (drink Royal Crown cola), and below, neon paraphs of orange and blue advertised Busch, Budweiser, Michelob and Coors. In the black storefront windows, amid depictions of frothing golden mugs of beer, some olives on toothpicks, pennanted squiggles meant to be eighth notes and crotchets, and green shamrocks, all in a child's hand.

Maybe, thought Roskilde, remembering the Shamrock Bar far, far away; deep in a golden silver dreamland desert on a dim olivaster planet in the Califia galaxy, where his father passed out checks to his crew of carpenters, laborers and mud slinging men (masons, cement mixers) on Friday nights a long time ago.

A lost away team of one, maybe he could do something about his unspared sobriety in that pub on the hill cap corner, out of the cold wind thrumming in the intersecting spider legs of the high wires.

Mare didn't drink, and stayed at the house. She tried to dissuade Roskilde from going into Packy Innard's, but he went, rationalizing that he was tornado bait, a peasant bumpkin spawn of rednecks, that it was this (in part) that got him 86'd, barred from the isle of the blest! Somewhere along the curvilinear way he'd mutated too much to fit though, even in Packy's; cursing welfare, middle management, etc. No, never had fit in. Working stiff, though.

What if the world once again turned to rend one of its heroes, and there was nobody there; merely the foggy dew, *(Apocalypsis cum figuris)* drinking beer in Packy Innard's Place?

He began to drop in to Packy's on his way to catch the ramshackle bus to work, on the corner, to down a couple in quick succession, wetting his whistle for the long shift (7:30 p.m. to 8:00 a.m.) ahead. Neverminding his inexorable *(Rosa Pocalypso)* fate, Churlemagne's ideology of gender, his vast boy choir, in rude health and partisan invective; becoming just one of the dumb topers in a quaint shebeen.

Everything about Packy Innard's Place had a homemade, old-fashioned look. The rough white surface of its exterior, the iron elbow mounts for the groaning air conditioner, the paunchy screen door, dart and egg molding around the ceiling, neon signage and vertical blinds in the black windows, to the plump salmon bumper along the bar, patched here and there with rhomboids of bone-gray duct tape.

Publican Packy Innard seemed an alert and genial social chieftain, tending his clientele, gossipy and charismatic in the Irish way. His mind seemed to mirror clearly the *mise en scène* which mirrored his mind. Roskilde witnessed Packy's opinions become law in that place organically; natural as a grapevine. Appeared Stalag San Antone and Packy Innard's Pub had this in common: they were havens of aboriginal mind, featuring hyperlinked alcoholic bush telegraphs of incredible instancy.

"Landlocked" barely survives as a category, but it applies to Sovere Hollow, the clachen of Awoken, Stalag San Antone, and Packy Innard's Place; the mind in there, its brain-ends mappable.

The first guy he met in Packy Innard's was Van Brunt, a loud, laughing, YY-chromo trucker. He was almost deferential to Roskilde, at first, but Roskilde knew it wouldn't last; brief honeymoon before a servo-mechanized campaign to dominate, exauctorate, all other items of mortality. They chatted amicably. *"I can tell you're smart,"* offered Van Brunt. The thing was, Roskilde had always known too much, just beyond the conversation. On this particularly luckless planet, that was a perilous facility. Triumphalists *(cupiditas principii)* of all stripes became covertly or openly murderous immediately upon noticing it. For now these were fast friends.

They shot a couple of games of eight ball, Packy looking on. When Roskilde won, Van Brunt called him a shark. Roskilde didn't exactly throw the next round, he just didn't try focused, and Packy smiled at his playing nice. Some more home boys came in.

Packy looked to be late middle-aged. Beef-stolid bigot, a commonplace in Sovere Hollow, but not in the aggressive style of Van Brunt, more in the manner of a landholding Afrikaner of Boland, or the Transvaal, it came to Roskilde. Sleeve garters would have suited Mr. Innard; he wore golf shirts, over an ideal beer belly. Planished, businesslike pewter hair, a slightly boss-eyed red mug, the faintest tremor of incipient Parkinson's Disease. He drank behind his bar methodically, contemplating the shrimpeyed bubbles rising as he peppered his beer, and never appeared drunk.

Roskilde squinted around his own silver Busch to absorb on Packy's impassive Irish countenance the same all-encompassing 100 yard beer stare his old Dad had employed to take in an entire barroom, with its gabbling denizens; this one's plumbing skills, that one's Yankee handyman expertise, and each and every conversation.

It's an underwater gaze, fixed on nobody in particular, dreaming but alert, relatively fool proof in boozy clairvoyance. Roskilde too was liable to go into that gaze, for the inclement overview.

Nobody notices. Time to go on in to work.

SECTION TWO

———

I *walk on in to a workplace I'll tell you about, through streets
from which the sense of ease, cheerfulness, and spontaneity is
vanishing. Or is it me?*

*Well, winter is getting here. A cold breeze swells beneath a
moving blue and black leopardskin sky, portentous of snow.*

*I find the keys, enter the back way, grab a sackful of fish fillets
from the freezer, and lay them out on an oven tray.*

*Professionally cheering up, I flip on the Arbus-eyed monitor and
set up for the night, putting out the hopeful stack of white towels.*

*Marisol Rosaura is shivering at the door. I click her in, followed
by Kaspar Hauser, rowdy old Micajah Harpe, and some of the boys
from Burgess Shale Camp on the river.*

*About a baker's dozen tonight; plenty of fish to go around. Set
out with loaves, supper commences.*

*Set the television low, and absorb talk from the soylent couch as
I tend to duties. . . overheard how in the sky, faint stars are crushed
like roses in a bible, into black holes. They say that frogs, with their
sensitive skins, are disappearing all over the world. . .*

*Impose a little order on the closet. Nachfalter will continue this
Augean thing in there, come Saturday.*

Review Menhaden's log entries. I've come to appreciate his style.

Chapman has somehow retrieved Marisol's lost luggage. She's pleased, and avers that Chapman owns and operates a heart of gold. There is some evidence for this.

Marisol is working, so we hold her bed. I'll try and interview Micajah tonight. Nachfalter taught me the armature of this job: to hold out a firm welcoming hand.

Called in, I'm learning the mission: to actually implement their Christ's social teachings with compassionate diligence.

Human or alien warmth passed hand to hand in St. Anthony's Haven, on a street of Awoken, down here far below the gridlocked traffic of the homeless stars.

Phone
LANGANS
ZIMA

SECTION THREE

"Warm Glimmer: A New Species?"

— CHARLES PLYMELL

The muggy summer lazily turned rainy. Roskilde had a cold that wouldn't go away. Walked raincoated into work, about half a block behind a group of his younger bums; disheveled mullet-cuts in baggy army surplus greatcoats, aimless paletots on grafts of blistered flour tortilla, flounder flesh and whitefish skin, frayed sheetrock sleeves, shiny over dirty spirit gum and tacky collodian, weaving through clinging streets in a jasta shoal, glassy-winged sharpshooters, lip sinking the passers by.

He opened, prepared tripe with hominy, and made a trifle of canned fruit cocktail over tough cookies, yellowcake, a few shriveled old candied green cherries, and Cool Whip. Micajah Harpe, looking waterlogged, but with a raptor's eye, in fruity, diabetic breath, uttered:

"I like it hard you know, sir. I like cold rain right in the face, and getting down through my clothes. I'm used to tough luck."

Roskilde understood. Hard luck was his god. He recollected an old, high fever, standing in a jeweline luminosity of drenched trees.

Quitting time in West Ward. Jimmy Grice's pickup materializes in its slot. Dvorák the butcher's van, color of old blood, parks across the street. Roskilde, among the working stiff regulars, loons down at the bar, impatient to chug that first hop soda. All restive with bibesy, to buy a taste of unconsciousness in the common room.

Some beer distributor's rep has endowed Packy's with a bar clock. Featuring a round shimmering ultramarine face, as of fireworms spawning on the surface of the sea. A blue rosace thought Roskilde. Glad to see it.

Smoking like chimneys, silver beer cans before them on the sill of the window let into the partition between the bar and the pool room, Roskilde and Grice watched Packy and Van Brunt shoot nine ball. Roskilde leaned, stock still, like a half-standing mammoth with buttercups in its mouth, listening to Grice.

Glimpses of consciousness, lurid flashes of insight into their Machiavel:

"Packy's always gotta be controlling somebody ain't it?"

Nodding, suspiring smoke, Roskilde rolled his eyes clockwise. Hard upon uttering this true thing in Roskilde's ear, Jimmy Grice crossed a lonesome beer meridian into a region of jabbered curses, muttered growls, on out to grunts in no language, to slowly, deliberately, don his yellow golf windbreaker, and abruptly exit into the night. Every night of the world. Roskilde was off, so stayed late in Packy Innard's Place to talk unsolved mysteries with zealous Dvorák, butcher of opinions. These two non-teleological symposiasts touched on the subject of neoteny.

One joker suggested neoteny theory might lay to rest some of the mystery concerning those interchangeable tabescent greys, and their scary unknowable agenda. How about their physical proportions? Their absence of neck hair and pigment in tissue cells? Their sexorgan diminution? The head to pelvis anomaly, (which might cast light on their seeming interest in artificial birthing). Their knowing too much just beyond the conversation? Their association with humanlike nearmen? Fetal and ancestral characteristics? Life forms of punctuated equilibria?

Roskilde, seeing his interlocutors draw a blank stare, warped on over to (zealots are poor listeners) materialized psychisms? Beings little over a yard tall spindly mantis sticks and outsize inverted pear cranials gray-green complected like smooth watered-on clay featuring wet obsidian pupil irisless wraparound great slant cat eyes over tiny nostrils and slit scar-mouth captors, whose cartilaginous long three or six fingered hands glide foot-long silver pencils lit at one end all over the body, and pushing up your stool?

"Jesus dewes. Do you know everything?
 How seriously have you researched this thing?"
"I'm a terrestrial, I belong to cofos."
"What's that?"
"Chromium oreos from outer space."

Packy watched the black specks in his beer. Dvořák didn't bat an eye. (Roskilde drank up, sighed deeply and walked on home, laughing, roaring with sorrow, rebalancing his head and oreopithecus). Bearing in his bodily frame the ineluctable stamp of his provenance.

Distant, muffled pops from the cemetery across Field Lane.

Wind blew rain lashing almost sideways in a freakishly vindictive cloudburst, furring in splintering silver the burnt orange brick facades of the Oktobryskaya, as Roskilde conceived of the big humped complex of buildings which, in the bowels of its cavernal basements housed Stalag San Antone.

He put together a kind of ur-chowder of tuna and mexi-corn, setting the pot to simmer on the stove. He straightened up, placing the Gideon bible and the A.A. book wide open on their respective end tables. He clicked on the silent T.V. and dusted. Running his hand between the cushions of the funkedelic green couch, he felt a sharp pain in his finger; he'd found a dirty (#3) hypodermic needle the hideous way. He tossed the needle, scrubbed his hands, and finished up preparations wearing rubber gloves, something he never neglected to do thereafter.

He opened a little early, hustling everyone quickly down off the street, forgoing one-on-one interviews in the foyer. Shapeless, squishing shoes. The drenched crush milled around, or squelched there in front of his station. Appalled, dripping rain, quivering, hair plastered to skulls. At the back of the shape up, Marisol was crying. All gazed wonderingly at Roskilde, as he looked back at them, brightening and fading; he was looking for something in their eyes. His search engine and flashlight loved the absence of predatoriness in a countenance, if another, unknown, unheard of thing could be sensed deep beneath the surface, like ancient martian water.

Met faces of astonished homelessness, in the frail respite of the Stalag San Antone shelter. He breathalyzed nobody that evening. Silently all signed the roster. Rain in gusts hammered the window. Commensal hands cupped bowls of hot soup, amazed. Thunder prowled outside. Supper was quiet, but for the idiot clapping of the wind.

Wipe to West Ward, interior of Packy Innard's Place. A pulpous unionid called Lehigh followed Roskilde into the tiny *(le water)* john, and leaning over his shoulder, watched him take a leak. Just checking, I guess, sighed Roskilde, and bought the scout a hard boiled pickled egg with a purple hairline crack in it, thinking (not in words): The yolk and glair of wisdom contained in the fable of the goose that laid the golden (curate's) egg is beyond these of the vicinity. The tragedy of David's long shot too, for that matter.

Roskilde had for some time been letting go the parts of his acculturated *(literae humaniores)* body petal by petal, organ by organ-stop, all over the hollow. At the bar in Packy Innard's Place, while nobody was watching, he released Bogart's weasand and frown.

Packy, who initially had taken a shine to Roskilde, and vetted his contingent new friends in the place, began to put the usual squeeze on; to get packaged, and settle into the pecking order. Roskilde's arm ached, his face felt red hot. Roskilde couldn't help but notice how several primal, postmodern traditions would rear ugly and alive in Packy Innard's Place, under the over-arching tall poppy syndrome, as it is known down under. Ascything down to size, to below sea-level. Smart-aleck cusk bludgeoned by gudgeons; recidivists lopped. Roskilde gut-felt when he was no longer exempt in there. (His nostalgia, memories of the long lost highways and shimmering electrum deserts of a remote planet to the southwest seemed to be borne to him on cold aqua velva eddies from the clock.)

Packy Innard's, no place to get uppity in.

Roskilde sat quietly, drinking beer, gazing into the busy luster of the stargush orbicle clock, a mexican electric azure sky seething through a darker, more slowly boiling, horse's eye purple.

Under the weird clock, a speckled trout whose tail would slap on a plaque, when its button was pushed. Other teetotems lurked around, and could be jolted alive, as if blue woad in a riptide effused these geegaws, and stained the water-pict faces of assembled churls, nickering, screaming unforgivable insults in one another's face. Ludicrously crowing.

Roskilde thought maybe one could trace this *(ultimi barbororum)* mockery to the fathers, the old-time anthracite miners, always in adrenaline derangement just to be able to stick their jobs; muscling into the earth down dangerous tunnels shored by unstable posts, then misery trudging home in company, a gang of other poor bastards like themselves, shining self-loathing into the coal-streaked faces of their brethren, with a shout. *"Ya piece of shit, ya!"* and that laughter, hopeless and violent. Quitting time. Sink a reeking, hot shot glass of amber whiskey to the bottom of a mug of yellow beer. Bet on stewball. Throw darts. Cruelly ride the spuriously male.

During an early visitation, can of Busch held low, Roskilde punched up a selection on the moldy jukebox: *"Every Christian Lion Hearted Man Will Show You"* by the Bee Gees. Instant consternation; Packy himself strode over, reached around in the back of the machine, and hit the reject button! Game meat of the semi ghost steeled itself.

Roskilde didn't much care to linger in Packy Innard's Place any longer, arguing with some jamoke's thalamus, indulging in counterintuitive behavior, smoking dromedaries, in a nightmare on Field Lane. The homes had this in common with Roskilde: only in dreams had they gone wrong. In Stalag San Antone, he was in charge and wasn't called upon to appear bigoted and dense. In fact, that would have been dangerous in there. Down in that reservoir of societal sky, a strict new polestar. He couldn't wait to catch the phaëton.

Sign in, supper, showers, interviews for the work programs 'til eleven. The veteran homeless knew to go to bed; the cherries by example. Then that grotto grew quiet. Eerie, sorrowing trains coupling, shunting in the switching yards way overtown, soft coughing from the barrack of retired souls. Roskilde sat at the desk, reading (Emil Cioran, François Villon, Fritz Perls, *Unicus* Magazine), or making entries in the night book. If an after hours conversation stirred in the sad saporous dark, he walked in, sighing deeply, to the muttering bunks and told them to shut up. Quasars and satellites are beyond our reach. The flood is over our heads. He opened a window and returned to his longueurs. *Grievous distant diesel whistles, and thin horn screams with dying falls.*

He staggered in dead on his feet and collapsed across the rich lap of his Madonna, where she sat doing bills on the loveseat in the parlor. Slept there for a minute eternity while she gazed expressionless onto his face, hushing the shouts of autochthons clangingly emptying garbage cans into growling, digestive trucks in the lane.

Leery friendliness of the ordinaries. Carnassial gleams, in the vermiculating blue dimness under the asterism writhing on the wall. The angelic little girl who collects for the newspaper appears silently at the bar. Drunks cajole her to speak but she never does.

One Saturday another drifter strayed into Packy Innard's Place. A dark, strapping marmalade, no, tortoise shell, no, brindle cat, perhaps from out the fields, or an anthracite-dark alameda somewhere. A mystery to human being, as cats are. Visitant who doesn't come when called. Packy fed it kippered herring, and adopted that surly stray or vice versa, and named it Deucey. Deucey was alien and self contained. Gnostic envoy. Not a buddhist, but Buddha, the gun slinger hick gunslingers dread. Deucey walked directly to Roskilde, curled in his lap there on a barstool and went right back to sleep.

Jostling prosimians loudly advised Packy as to whether or not he should keep that cat, each according to his lights. Those for Deucey earned stars in Roskilde's book; those who snarled that Deucey should be shut out, or crueler, put to death, he also noted. Several jamokes to whom Deucey was immediately averse earned Roskilde's dubiety too. All kept their own counsel, cards to the vest, belly to the bar, but who among them was a right ailurophile?

The joint was growing stiffer, ever more hostile; beer didn't cheer

Roskilde up, like it used to. He observed surreptitiously, with a jaundiced eye. The boys wore their caps backward; the men turned them back around. As we have seen, it wasn't only ball caps or forage caps atop every roundhead, it was something mute, brute and pervasive that made these dragoons resemble one another so closely, shoulder to shoulder, cheek by jowl along the fabrikoid orange cuff. Not only his capless, pruinose topknot set Roskilde quite apart:

Out the window, under a mean lime witness moon, the lanes across the hollow slept all unaware, while Roskilde grew forever wider awake, and it was rubbing him out the wrong way.

Looks like the light, hopeful and difficult country and western pie had been off all along, he mused. Down here in the hollow the proletariat existed as Churlemagne preferred Roskilde die: everything and nothing. A new van. Tomato festivals, truck pulls, casseroles for supper. Endlessly futile golf. Stupid, vulgar poppy lopping, projected self-contempt. *"If you were anybody, you wouldn't even know me."* *(Le water)*, beer chasing out beer, each and everyday into the evening. Received (of whom?) opinions. Worship of sport champions, (with the exception of the intelligent Tiger Woods.) Every gossiping male body attuned to hearsay, with sinistral english personally put on each cheap shot. In the matter of village deaths eagerly reported, each churl a shameless cradle catholic ghoul. Roskilde avorton a sewer lily on high lager rising? Feel so break up, he want to go home. Phantom Clove. Titivil, stick a fork in him, he's done. His passion had ever tended to roar up to blue heat only to damp down and then out, even to a pilot light. He knew this would get him killed. A ringlet of fog lingered round his loins. Another beer here. This is no ordinary hollow of lostness; here is a boiled-down compression hole of the hells, simply black with muddy chicken-shit. The defense wrests.

SECTION FOUR

———

*"To wail the fault you visualize. What form would
surface with an explosive separate being,
desperate last chance?"**

— W.S. BURROUGHS

Roskilde was glad to take off to the shelter. In general, the have-nots crying uncle in there were sweeter-natured by far, and less enchained than the blue collars of Innard's *Thing*. Less hateful, even many who were doomed to die of awareness. The exceptions to the rule were as spasm standoffs or runaway viruses. These are property?

Since the homeless were not competitive for cushy slots, or the boss's ear, as those in the jobbing world tend to be, they seldom evinced that compulsive jokiness which masks an Iscariot-like hierarchy of killer climbing monkeys just kidding, quite so egregiously. These were world-poor, reacting to things. They have come to eat, I suppose. In Packy's place the aggressive jape raved, on the lip and the bite, in the buy. Your disenfranchised aren't serious, when they play the dozens. *"Monkey feather, you so dumbfounded if they moved your tray six inches, you'd starve to death."* The desolation from which a night in the haven distracted them, came flooding back on the stark morning street, Roskilde knew. By next evening it was in spate, far as eye could see. Once more then, sighing, Roskilde opened the sluice, joking and scolding, to hot supper, showers, white clean towels, television, repose.

* *From The Western Lands, Printed in the USA By Haddon Craftsmen, Scranton, PA.*

He made a good shepherds' pie with diced gammon, something he learned over in London, where he saw in a shop window an odd thing: A mannequin of Henry VIII in black leather biker livery. (Mute fat marbling Brando's hams) His homeless charges spoke with shock and awe of an x-ray vision, brought to bear as an afterburner of personal histories, or lies. Roskilde saw through them, as Churlemagne weedwhacker crowed he saw through Roskilde's dewy form, broken down at phaserpoint to the mare beneath the kid, plumb down to a stick insectile fairy skinny dipping in a cesspuddle at the bottom of the terrene orchestra pit. Further, to a famished wraith of wind on the other side of things, then nothing, black vacuum of outer space. Where he was coming from, fluid became turbulent, with roaming charges.

Roskilde imparted to castaways clues to the open and shut skies; supposedly implicated in keeping their tragic carnival on the road, as god's fool he moved heaven and earth for them, swapping ends in the matter of ignorant despair and fatuous hope (desponder, transponder) without fostering further corporeality, nor emboldening turtledoves, crybaby Cujos or their fawning vinchucas to hanker after what was not for them: to "make it" in any given hell. Acted out for them on smoking waters, stair-danced on wormy air; was seen moon walking briskly back into the upper atmosphere, off world.

Then, one glittering bluish morning after the sexton watch, with Colonel Al Kern, Eugene Podkletnov and Barbelo in tow, careering through the cruel chill on Ash Street toward the Yar Bar and Grill for a breakfast of flat beer, Roskilde's heart suddenly attacked him, dashing him viciously to the pavement, smashing his brow. A tiny ambulance, in shrill pain, sped him away to Pity Hospital where he lay intubated doggo for three days. Tests found Hepatitis C contaminating a rent heart, under fresh stitches and wet scabs. Cut to the brain.

Mortified, Roskilde climbed on hands and knees upstairs to bed. No nest egg, no specie in the hamburger sparkasse. Drawing on a bank of fog against drifting apart, where the sun leaves and returns.

Roskilde, he, she, it, was zwieback.

Here was the thing too terrible to be true. Roskilde's liver, formerly the cock's comb, felt hollow. His heart ached when she coughed, watching the skies. A vast exhausted Aeolian skinner wheezed in immense, clotted cumulus clouds peopled by the tumbling departed. Durance of those rows of cirro-cumuli under sail up yonder, less than a mortal hour, thought Roskilde. Unimaginably far sothic stars went cross-eyed, and here was an antivenin to inspiration; it meant to leave him only her moldering body, his stupid sepulture. Cool mammate chryselephantine thorax calamitously sprent with red rain spider angiomas. Hell of Woman down there.

Just as he had been left by soldiers of the pack-like whelm of *(lycopithecus)* victors, Roskilde himself was taking his leave of that violently ignorant place, the troke body, monkey vase of history, regarding it with disdainful equanimity over the whispered wing of a shoulder, behind him on the ground. Spirit unfolds itself alone on Mars.

He strove, sweating blood, to boot strap the Roskilde out from the lake of fire. He laughed a wintry laugh: even if he had delired his entire tape up to now. Even if stupidity, cowardice, blinky milk of amnesia, had tried to get away with patronizing the real. Impossible spine aching in a vegetative pie, beneath proof to the contrary, beyond deliquescent beads of tapioca (now photons), nuclear winterland, past that, in turnip winter, beyond doubt, beyond belief. Blood-surround of a neutron rose, beyond reason or device.

Agonic and retrieved, Roskilde had attained critical opalescence, with the lion face. An ornate moth lifted its twayblade eyes to a streaming wound, in the recognition he'd received it long ago.

It was the Sun.

So, he dug and planted a knot garden near the back door. Distant mole hills of afternoon shone like bronzing powder on cleavage. Babbage, zucchini, collards, ashberys, an jalapeño bush, salary, and for the stubborn herd fear and sturdy glandular homogeneity which cannot leave the human animal killer race, yellow tomatoes and little albino eggplants, like flash bulbs.

He found a wooden chair in the street, sat down in it beside his garden, with a squirrel and a starling, and rested. On the knee high scalloped white wire fence, the twining morning glory, blooming heavenly lavender, pale red, with heart shaped leaves for humans and beings. Bees ministered to squash blossoms un-spun in the sun.

He set the wrack of cast-off chair beside the slouching garden, sat down in it with a sigh, and composed a last human ballad. After awhile, the hermit sang it to the empty neighborhood:

"Farewell my portrait of the Prima Vera,
goodbye my smoky star,
adios indelible picture
so long my heart's desire.

For the mirror empties into morning,
& the clouds leak glittering snow,
& the dark bright light torments me,
as the sun is sinking low.

Yes the sky tortures me sweetly
as the cows are walking home,
& the swallows are returning,
& arrives the fiery gloam.

No woman can release me
so my shiny craft can leave,
& the gnarled moon ignores me
as they're bringing in the sheaves.

O leafy path through the Prima Vera
beneath a high green star,
be quenched in oblivious music,
so long my lute & lyre."

The dozy packing effect of the virus was *almost* irenic. Roskilde labored mornings in the dripping garden, toward distant evenings when he could make his way into gigantic sleep, and be alright.

The child, fletcher to the man, gravely aimed at slumber for that tired kid. The blue candlewick quilt is down, but oblivion is the ultimate comforter.

Roskilde, in the garden, thought of his homeless; their big rock candy mountain which didn't exist, and himself as some kind of Rafael Lemkin for the Hounds of Tindalos. Vain! Touched his wound, his executed, field dressed and jerked dream he dwelt in marble halls.

Hearken to the mourning doves; soft blue crying calls expressing what swells with silence in the embattled, astigmatic soul.

Veraguth's fold; The lesser doughnut was flat. Across the hollow, the stations. An illuminated shell at a crossroads. Punk neon ghosts of the great Himself. Naked leg syndrome of a rose bush blighted by trash dump traces. That gry, tuned and shining clitoris of Edna St. Vincent Millay.

Thus life returned with dawn, just the slightest lilt. Then he would walk out along the lanes in the weather; sunny, or under great cobalt cloud folds, amassments of lowering shade moving over moldering, particle-boarded up deadlights of Awoken Lace, next to the foundry in Leakey Industrial Park; an abandoned handball court with a stagnant little central rain pond echoing his footfalls, factory buildings, then lawn order box habitations, a fleet of silhouettes unto the outer limits, through vacant lots rank with Kong sunflowers, shriveled or blooming plastic scumbags caught on burdock, milkweed, joe-pye, dewberry briars and nettles, cream bells of strumpet vines specked with frass, curly over cinerous peppercorn ground around dewy toads mimicking clods and stones. Coprolites, lithics? (Bukowski's unspeakable lower intestine.)

In the matter of the ten thousand things, Churlemagne had impeached Roskilde for devouring edicarp surfaces and spitting out the putamens; for emboldening his pretty mind (and heart) to see a protagonist (and antagonist) in the mountainscape, heathscape, and across the swept up hollows.

Studies of black holes seem to show that, although it defies common sense, the maximum entropy or information content of any region of space is defined not by its volume but by its surface area. (*Scientific American, August 2003*).

Roskilde had found the narrow path through the vacant lots (a bitter old tricycle in weeds) comely morning and evening; oscine alleys of Awoken, where shrikes are mewed up, becoming in shade, pregnantly mysterious, on the way to and from shelter.

At last tearing away (our Lady vanishes) from the clinging street birds, who snagged his heart in every lenient place on it, he'd loved walking alone to Westward under umbrageous colonnades of spruce sheer against the sky, swift chimney swifts, sober vesper bells, (which he need not ask for whom were tolling), the arched black iron comb of the Drubinick trestle, from which he beheld the wrecked bran pie of Awoken, puddled twinkling in its long depressions. Surely this way was the long one to have come,

Roskilde sighed.

Roskilde closed the circuit of his mosey at the peach-blow plastic sign over pickled, candescent Packy Innard's Place (from the other side). The familiar sign buoyed levigate in the morning breeze and seemed faintly aglow.

Surfaces. Don't they speak to you from depths, treeman? Don't they tell you what you long to know, those faces, the shiny, alien vans? That fleeting, bitter moue no barfly caught. . . infinite no? That cat asleep on the bar, serenity, time out of mind? Man's laughter, never to be trusted?

Trying the door, Roskilde was surprised to find Packy's open. Slightly ahead of himself, his dewy hologram did the dead cat bounce into the room and bade good morning to old Reggie Sprat, who was wiping the bar in circles.

"Where you coming from?" asked Sprat sourly.
"You look kinda green, sparky."
"Been walking the traces in this lost and nival vale."

"Speak English," said Sprat, setting a silver Busch before his first customer of the day. Sprat exactly resembled Andy Rooney, but for the light of kindly intelligence in the old journalist's eyes. Sprat had ossified pearl onion eyes.

Roskilde discovered alcohol now made him sick in a heartthrob, inextricably mingling the hangover into the first beers, making surfaces fascinating and sinister at once. From a stool by the window he gingerly sipped beer, gazing out on Field Lane, deserted at that hour, save for a dusty icebox-white Monte Carlo SS at the curb, featuring a fat sheaf of foxed, yellowed tickets swelling under a windshield wiper, and four flat tires.

Light as chaff, cagastrical, Roskilde suicidally drank beer into the afternoon, and the arrival of the ordinaries. A livepool filling one by one. The preposterous draught of fishes. Tremulous zircons (de Beer's) glide over walls of a Devonian grotto; fish-eyes wriggling from the ultramarine clock, under-beer cavern reflecting submarine vans, pickups, drag racing hoopties, a whopping, scarred oyster-white tractor and reefer oozing by in the lane, as beer idiotizes the features of each sleeping, staring face. His head swam.

Everything looked far away. Packy seemed to lead a cigar antennuled camarilla into the room and relieve Sprat behind the bar. Lone Roskilde dreaming of these white Christians, and the rapture on coyote day. Clink of darbies in a box of white owls. Someone, Packy or Reggie, caused the chipper gopher to chirp *"I'm alright,"* rocking its revolting little head. The teddy-Elvis-gorilla slurringly intoned *"Hunka Hunka Burnin' Love."* A brace of bakelite bulldogs atop the beer cooler began to bark. Porcelain baskel meowed her arch counterpoint. Deucey flashed out the back.

Packy had taken a deep seat opposite Roskilde. He seemed out of spirits and had a blind-sight look, stricken and determined, frowning at Roskilde but somehow up to one side, like a governor on a poster. He seemed to be piloting him out of his place, with that owner's decisiveness which renders one at least three times as obsolete as the Tridentine Mass, or diaper pails.

Sighing, Roskilde drank in silverback Packy Innard's alpha tropism to dominion (in hard stratagems fashioned good naturedly man and boy and two uncommonly sharp seeing eye teeth). Near his elbow, a winter fly washed its microscopic hands.

A brutish subconscious rendering of an ancient thing served here. A rotten state. Resistance is futile. Indistinct background frieze scrum along the bar, a slavering, bobbling, dozen-headed douzeper.

Juddering blue light fell from the starry clock over Packy's bust. The black hollows of his eye sockets turned his countenance into the

Sutton Hoo Helmet.

It was Churlemagne.

As Roskilde closed the storm door of Packy Innard's shebang behind him and stepped out onto pavement of Field Lane, whitening as if with castor sugar, there was a loud pop, and from the filling boneyard across the way a puff of pinkish smoke rose in a rolling ball that quickly dissolved in the falling snow.

He descried, down the lane, His Madonna, holding a palm up to the cold falling petals. He called to her as she ducked into their house and caught up with her as she re-emerged with a candy stripe umbrella, unfurling it. She appeared much taller than he.

"I was coming to fish you out of that place, man."
"Wetter inside all the time, Mare. What's shaking?"
"Just wanted to let you know I'm leaving.
Pour beer on your liver.
I'll catch you on the weekend."
"I be dog. That was my last time in there though."
"Right. Feed the cat and vacuum will you?
White hair over every
fucking inch of everything. You shed too."

Mare left him standing on the porch. Forsaken, he watched her red tail lights receding, braking, receding, down Field Lane. He listened to the alarming, silent clock of snow in yards, on roofs, drifting in gutters over all Westward. It was a filthy night; the night before Christmas, beginning to snow harder. In the flickering perse of parlors sat the humans of the hollow; uncouth beings, stomachers of an olden time, ungainly citizens grunting in repose, torpid, besotted, lulled plumb down to the golf course, salved with a variety of river dances, bear and bull baitings, and utterly pedestrian sitcoms on T.V. All this spaced out by holidays (troll what a somehow infernal, gaudy display of Yuletide decorations strung sputtering everywhere across the vicinage, each habitation and plot a blazing bramble of fairy-flame corn, eval rows of fake zig-zag icicles, a flood-lit crèche, neon spiral conifers, a goblin fruit Santa bending to a hookah-smoking caterpillar

(!?) Opaque plastic wreaths and huge bows amid dotty torsades and ellipses of diminutive bulbs winking red, sparking blue, shorting out in the eddying snow strobing greenish, voidical). . .

Through each season of planeticose becoming, from the forever opening rose, he had fallen for that mysterious thing in earth's *(locus squalus)* situation; heaven ruining from heaven, down the mountainsides, eddies carried by larger eddies from glen to glen, and petal by petal possident realtors, bearing the ape salt, liquidated Roskilde.

He rose through the falling snow free, as if he had not existed. Ignorant deputies dragged the river.

Where present hour Batterman Avenue honks and crosses Ash Street, once stood owl quaver wilderness. Right there the Sovere brothers, Clovis and Newcomb, cleared a spot whereon to raise sheep. Depredations of lank wolves and big cats from out Lambeth Mire finished off their poor flock. A long khaki tract of rye swayed where Drubinick station stands now.

A squire Westermark, at a meeting of the backwoods Thing, sold the Sovere boys his grist mill there in 1797. It was known to early settlers as Gnarlymoon Glen, from the contours of its surrounding hills, I suppose, with a worldweary breeze through a weald of scrub boscage pine, tanoak, hemlock, and near the heart of that place, a gigantic Norway oak. The breeze passes away, day spent to a last red cent of sun. Such quiet in shady groves and on the wooded hills. Stalled echo of a far axe in a dell. Forest murmurs. Nightfall.

No traveler on Warrior Trail, winding down from Zealand. Would you believe sky men (from out of space) alighting on hilltops so gently as to stay unbeknownst, who watch for a twinkling, then regain their flyby trajectories?

By and by the fields and pasture around the great oak shading a rude grain mill and distillery, became known as Sovere Hollow, and many a poor boy rode a mule up to that still, to charge his jugs with the burning usquebaugh.

ABOUT THE AUTHOR

David Omer Bearden is the surviving brother of twins born in the desert town of Blythe, CA in 1940. He dedicated his creative life to writing poetry, starting from the post-Beat era, until he passed away in 2008 in Scranton, Pennsylvania. From 1958-1962 he studied English Literature at the University of Tulsa, where he discovered the writings of the "Beats" and began publishing his own poems in numerous literary magazines and journals. Bearden was also a fiction writer, publisher, composer, traveler, and musician who shared a deep and poetic romance with singer/songwriter Judee Sill. *The Thing In Packy Innard's Place* was the last manuscript he completed in 2007. He is also known as the "Apocalypse Rose."

To learn more about the author visit: davidbearden.com